Hurry, Murray, Hurry!

Library of Congress Cataloging-in-Publication Data

Keeshan, Bob.

Hurry, Murray, hurry! / Bob Keeshan ; illustrations by Chad Peterson.

p. cm.

Summary: Although nine-year-olds Murray and Henrietta usually take life slowly in a society where others rush, they know that some things must be done quickly if the environment is to be protected.

ISBN 0-925190-84-5 (hc : acid free)

[1. Time—Fiction. 2. Environmental protection—Fiction.] I. Peterson, Chad, ill. II. Title.

PZ7.K2513Hu 1996

[Fic]—dc20 95-40505

CIP

AC

First printing: October 1996

Printed in the United States of America

00 99 98 97 96 7 6 5 4 3 2 1

Published by Fairview Press, 2450 Riverside Avenue South, Minneapolis, MN 55454.

For a current catalog of Fairview Press titles, please call this Toll-Free number: 1-800-544-8207.

Cover design by Circus Design

Publisher's Note: Fairview Press publishes books and other materials related to the subjects of family and social issues. Its publications, including *Hurry, Murray, Hurry!* do not necessarily reflect the philosophy of Fairview Hospital and Healthcare Services or their treatment programs.

The paper used in this publication meets the minimum requirements of American National Standard for Information Sciences—Permanence of Paper for Printed Library Materials, ANSI Z329.48-1984.

Hurry, Murray, Hurry!

Bob Keeshan

illustrated by Chad Peterson

Fairview Press
Minneapolis, Minnesota

To my grandchildren, whom I hope will never
hurry through childhood

Murray was nine years old. He was in no hurry to be ten. He liked being nine and knew he would be ten sometime in the next year. Murray was in the third grade, and he was in no hurry to get to the fourth grade. He knew that would happen soon, but he enjoyed the third grade.

Murray enjoyed being nine and enjoyed being in the third grade because he liked the things he saw every day and he liked the things he did every day. It seemed to Murray that everyone around him, his classmates and the grown-ups, were always rushing. Murray did not like to rush. He liked to take his time doing things and seeing things and hearing things and touching things and taking slow, deep breaths of fresh air. Murray enjoyed being Murray.

All around him people were rushing. Quick! do this. Quick! do that. Let's get on our way. Good, we are here. Now, let's leave. Let's go. Now! Rushing. People were always rushing and looking back and saying, "Hurry, Murray. Hurry!"

Everyone rushed except his friend from the third grade—Henrietta. Henrietta was also nine years old and she enjoyed taking her time to do things and see things and hear things and touch things, and she enjoyed taking slow, deep breaths of fresh air. Henrietta enjoyed being Henrietta.

Henrietta's brother said she had been named Henrietta because it was a slow name. It took a long time to say:

Hen-ri-et-ta.

It took so long to say that people started to call her Harry, for short. People seemed to like taking shortcuts. They called her Harry and were always rushing and were always looking back and saying, "Hurry, Harry. Hurry!"

In school, Murray and Harry were good friends. Every week, their teacher gave the class a test. The test was called "multiple choice." Murray and Harry liked to think about these tests, and they took their time deciding the correct answers. The last question on the test looked like this:

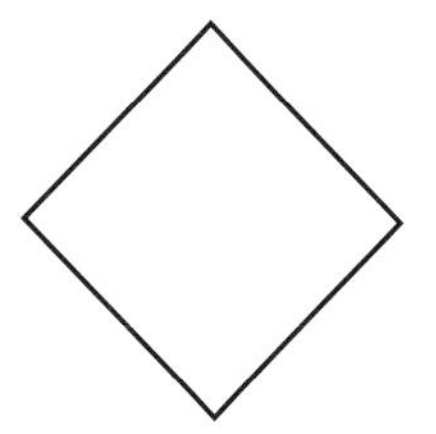

This shape is known as a:
(a) square
(b) diamond
(c) triangle
(d) musical instrument

The other kids were all in a big hurry to finish the test. They would look at the question and say: "Is it (a), (b), (c), (d)? Oh, quick—I want to be done early. I'll guess at one."

Soon, all the kids except Harry and Murray were finished with their tests and rushed their papers to the teacher's desk. Whoosh! As they passed, they would whisper in a LOUD WHISPER, "Hurry, Murray! Hurry, Harry!"

Time was almost up. Tick, tock, tick, tock, went the clock on the wall above the chalkboard. Harry and Murray kept on working until it was almost time for the bell to ring.

Almost. Just before the bell, Murray and Harry got up and handed their test papers to the teacher. As she took them in her hand, the bell RANGGGGG!

The next day, the teacher handed out the corrected papers. And guess what? Murray and Harry were the only kids to get perfect scores.

A

It wasn't that Murray and Harry always did things slowly. Some things had to be done in a hurry. They knew that. When they played baseball after school they knew how to hurry. When Murray hit the ball into center field, he knew he had to hurry to first base, maybe even hurry to second.

Harry played the outfield—right field and right-center field (because they didn't have anyone to play center field). So, if someone hit a long fly to right-center field, Harry had to hurry, hurry, hurry, and RUNNNN to make the catch. She was fast.

One time, Murray and Harry went to the Central Zoological Garden (the zoo) with their class. Everybody started to run around, going from one place to another, looking quickly at the birds, quickly at the fish, quickly at the seals, quickly at the elephants, quickly at the little monkeys, quickly at the great apes. They kept calling, "Hurry, Murray. Hurry, Harry. HURRRRYYY!"

But Murray and Harry just took their time, slowly looking at each animal and wondering. I wonder what he thinks of the zoo? I wonder what she likes to eat? Would he like peanut butter and jelly sandwiches as much as I do? Probably not.

Harry looked at the tigers for a long time. They had stripes and beautiful fur. They were very large. There were some baby tigers with the grown-up tigers. A sign said that these were Siberian tigers and that the babies had been born there at the zoo. Harry wondered where in the world Siberia was. One large tiger, with large eyes, looked right at her as though to say, "Harry, don't you know where Siberia is?"

Murray spent a long time with the orangutans. There was a sign near the fence around the orangutans' field. The sign said they came from Borneo and a small part of Sumatra. "Where in the world are those places?" thought Murray. Just then a large orangutan looked right at Murray. He was looking right into Murray's eyes. Maybe he was saying, "Murray, don't you know where Borneo is?"

When Murray got home that night, he asked his mother if he could look at the atlas. His mother said, "Of course, dear, it's here somewhere. . . ." Quickly she looked in one bookcase—top shelf, second shelf, third shelf, bottom shelf. Then, quickly to the next bookcase—

Murray said slowly, "Isn't that it, on the bottom shelf of the first bookcase?"

"Of course it is, dear. I was going so fast, I went right past it. Haste makes waste, they say."

Murray took the atlas and located Borneo, an island in southeast Asia. In the encyclopedia, Murray found "ORANGUTANS" and learned that they were an endangered species, mostly because people were building their houses where the orangutans had always lived. They were being pushed out of their homes. This made Murray sad.

BORNEO

Harry also was wondering about the animals at the zoo. She asked her brother where the encyclopedia was, but he hurried away to play. “I don’t have time to find it. I’m in a hurry!” he said as he raced out the door.

Harry finally found her encyclopedia and located Siberia, the natural home of the tigers she saw at the zoo. People were invading the tigers’ homeland, too. The Siberian tiger was an endangered species. She wished those little tigers could live freely in Siberia.

Siberia

After dinner, Murray's mom said, "Hurry, Murray, hurry!" It was time to do some shopping. "Hurry, Murray, hurry!"

At the supermarket, they met Harry, who was helping her father with the shopping. Soon, Murray and Harry were left in the dust as their parents whizzed through the aisles—up this aisle, down that aisle, across the back, then back across the front. This into the basket, that into the basket—whoosh, whoosh, hurry, hurry . . . got to get finished—quickly!

Harry and Murray stayed in the vegetable section and saw the different vegetables. They looked at all the colors. There were yellow onions and white onions, brown potatoes, green lettuce, lighter-green lettuce, and four different colors in the pepper section: green, red, yellow, and orange.

When their parents were at the checkout counter, Harry and Murray were told that they could each have an ice cream pop. The man at the checkout counter asked, "Do you want the ice cream wrapped, or are you going to eat it right away?"

"Bag it, please," said Harry. "It will taste better if I can think about it all the way home. Things seem to taste better if you wait a while before eating them."

"Me too," said Murray. "I'll wait. Bag it, please."

They each thought about the ice cream on the way home, and when they finally ate it, it tasted like the best ice cream ever.

"Waiting makes most things better," said Murray.

On the last day of school, the teacher said the class could eat lunch outside. The other kids had rushed through lunch and were playing tag and catch-me-if-you-can. Murray and Harry sat with the last part of their lunch—bags of crunchies, carrot sticks, celery, and slices of green pepper. They sat munching and talking about the animals from the zoo.

They each wished they were able to protect the tigers and orangutans and other animals on earth. They talked about the environment and what they could do to make their earth a better place for everyone, including tigers and orangutans. Harry and Murray decided that they would work on these problems as grown-ups, but for now, they were just kids. What could they do?

They finished the crunchies, threw the bags on the ground, and went to join the other kids in catch-me-if-you-can.

Almost together, Harry and Murray stopped and turned. They looked at the empty crunchie bags on the ground, picked them up, and put them in the trash can.

"We may not be able to do much about the tigers in Siberia, but we can do something to keep our neighborhood looking good," said Harry.

Murray and Harry brought their report cards home from school that day.

"Congratulations, Murray," said his mother. "You've been promoted to the fourth grade!"

"Great, son," said his dad. "It won't be long before you'll be in the fifth grade!"

"Dad, I'm not going to start the fourth grade until next September. I'm going to take the whole year to enjoy it. I will like being a fourth grader."

"Take your time, Murray," said his dad.

"Take your time, Murray," said his mom.

"Don't hurry, Murray. Don't hurry."

Harry also was promoted to fourth grade.

"In no time, you'll be eleven or twelve and in the sixth grade," said her mom.

"Yep," said her dad.

"Mom! Dad!" Henrietta yelled.

"Oops, we know. You're in no hurry," said her dad.

"So take your time and don't hurry," said her mom.

They both said, "Don't hurry, Henrietta. Don't hurry!"

Other children's books from Fairview Press

Alligator in the Basement, by Bob Keeshan, TV's Captain Kangaroo
illustrated by Kyle Corkum

Box-Head Boy, by Christine M. Winn with David Walsh, Ph.D.
illustrated by Christine M. Winn

Clover's Secret, by Christine M. Winn with David Walsh, Ph.D.
illustrated by Christine M. Winn

Monster Boy, by Christine M. Winn with David Walsh, Ph.D.
illustrated by Christine M. Winn

My Dad Has HIV, by Earl Alexander, Sheila Rudin, Pam Sejkora
illustrated by Ronnie Walter Shipman

"Wonderful You" Series, by Slim Goodbody
illustrated by Terry Boles
The Body
The Mind
The Spirit